Dear Parent:
Your child's love of reading starts here!

Every child learns to read in a different way and at his or her own speed. Some go back and forth between reading levels and read favorite books again and again. Others read through each level in order. You can help your young reader improve and become more confident by encouraging his or her own interests and abilities. From books your child reads with you to the first books he or she reads alone, there are I Can Read Books for every stage of reading:

SHARED READING
Basic language, word repetition, and whimsical illustrations, ideal for sharing with your emergent reader

BEGINNING READING
Short sentences, familiar words, and simple concepts for children eager to read on their own

READING WITH HELP
Engaging stories, longer sentences, and language play for developing readers

READING ALONE
Complex plots, challenging vocabulary, and high-interest topics for the independent reader

ADVANCED READING
Short paragraphs, chapters, and exciting themes for the perfect bridge to chapter books

I Can Read Books have introduced children to the joy of reading since 1957. Featuring award-winning authors and illustrators and a fabulous cast of beloved characters, I Can Read Books set the standard for beginning readers.

A lifetime of discovery begins with the magical words "I Can Read!"

Visit www.icanread.com for information
on enriching your child's reading experience.

For my daughter Paris,
who taught me just how
spooky a sleepover can be.
—D.K.

I Can Read Book® is a trademark of HarperCollins Publishers.

ISBN 978-0-06-085477-5 (pbk.) — ISBN 978-0-06-085478-2 (trade bdg.)

14 15 16 17 18   LP/WOR   10 9 8 7 6 5 4 3 2 1

❖

First Edition

READING
2
WITH HELP

MONSTER SCHOOL

THE SPOOKY SLEEPOVER

Written and illustrated by
DAVE KEANE

HARPER
An Imprint of HarperCollins*Publishers*

Norm was going to a sleepover.

He was very nervous.

It was his first time

sleeping away from home.

Norm wanted to bring too much.

This sleepover wasn't

at a friend's house.

It was at Norm's school.

All the kids were little monsters,

but that's not what worried him.

"I miss my bed already," said Norm.

NO HOWLING

Norm wasn't like the other kids.

He could not turn into a bat.

He did not howl at the moon.

Norm did not cry out of ten eyeballs.

He had only two.

Norm was just normal.

Norm's class had sold

the most at the school bake sale.

They had won a sleepover

in the library.

"Why does the prize

have to be so scary?" Norm asked.

Miss Grunt was the librarian.

She was nice, but she was a zombie.

"GRRRRRRRRRR!" she said.

This did not help Norm feel safe.

Miss Clops was Norm's teacher.

Norm had never seen a teacher

in her pajamas.

Her eye already looked sleepy.

Norm thought she might also

have an eye in the back of her head.

WHOA

15

"Story time!" Hilda yelled.

"Of course it is a spooky story,"

Norm mumbled.

Norm held his bunny tight.

Hilda hugged her salamander.

Bianca got in trouble

for talking to herself.

"Oh no! Gill fell asleep

already!" cried Frankie.

Gill snored through his gills.

"That is just gross," Norm said.

"Pizza time!" Gary shouted.

"Gary is here?" asked Norm.

"I can't see him."

"Ghosts are like that," said Hilda.

The pizza that Gary was eating fell

right to the floor. SPLAT!

"Hey, I am still hungry," said Gary.

Harry turned hairy.

He ate two whole cheese pizzas.

He ate the boxes, too.

"He will have bad dreams," Norm said.

"Movie time!" Hilda yelled.

"It is a scary movie,

of course," Norm muttered.

"Hey, look, that is

my uncle Walt!" said Vinnie.

Vinnie was so excited

that he turned into a bat.

Later, Norm brushed his teeth.

Other kids brushed their fangs.

One girl brushed her face.

A boy clipped his claws.

"That is a little rude," said Norm.

They got their sleeping bags ready.

Bianca forgot one of her pillows.

Elsa forgot her bunny slippers.

Isaac lost his fuzzy blanket

and cried his eyes out.

Mort's sleeping bag had sand in it.

"How can you sleep with sand?"

asked Norm.

"It reminds me of home," said Mort.

"I couldn't sleep with sand, or with a mouse in my head," said Norm. "Oh, it's the snake in my tummy that keeps me awake," said Mort.

Hilda, Bianca, and the other girls

played a trick on the boys.

Norm jumped up.

Mort's mouse ran away.

Vinnie flew home.

But Gill just kept snoring

through his gills.

Soon everyone settled down,

but Norm could not sleep.

He began to sniff.

Everybody asked him

what was wrong.

"I can't fall asleep.

I do not have my night-light.

My cat is not sleeping with me.

And my mother did not

hum a sweet tune for me."

29

"Oh, don't worry, Norm," said Gary.

"I can glow for you all night."

"And I can make a cat," said Hilda.

ZAP! She turned her salamander

into a cat that curled up

and went to sleep at Norm's feet.

"And I am an expert at humming

sweet songs," said Miss Clops.

She sat in Gary's glow

and hummed sweet songs for Norm.

Soon Norm smiled and closed his eyes.
Sleepovers can be scary, he thought,
but it sure helps to be surrounded
by some very good friends.